This book is dedicated with love to my brothers,
Joe and Rob, and their families.

two lions

Text and illustrations copyright © 2013 by Bill Thomson

Amazon Publishing
Attn: Amazon Children's Publishing
P.O. Box 400818, Las Vegas, NV 89140
www.amazon.com/amazonchildrenspublishing

Library of Congress Cataloging-in-Publication Data is available upon request.

ISBN-13: 9781477847008 (hardcover)
ISBN-10: 1477847006 (hardcover)
ISBN-13: 9781477897003 (eBook)
ISBN-10: 1477897003 (eBook)

Book design by Katrina Damkoehler
Editor: Margery Cuyler

Printed in Mexico
First edition
10 9 8 7 6 5 4 3 2 1

Bill Thomson embraced traditional painting techniques and meticulously painted
each illustration by hand, using acrylic paint and colored pencils.
His illustrations are not photographs or computer generated images.

A fossil shows the traces or remains of animals
and plants that lived 10,000 or more years ago.
A fossil can be a rock with a preserved part
of an extinct animal or the imprint of an
ancient plant. By studying fossils, we can
learn a lot about prehistoric life.

*In loving remembrance of the students and teachers
of Sandy Hook Elementary School.*

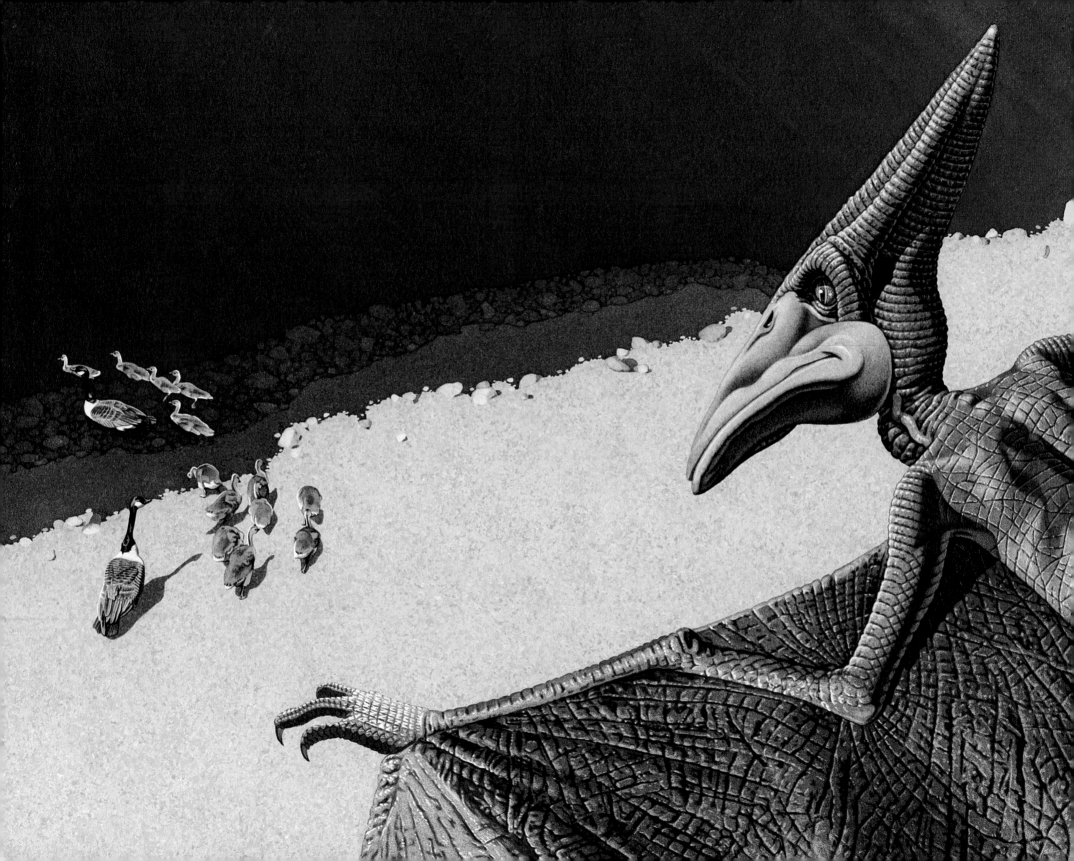